BABOU

THE BEAR

by

Monica Wallach

There once was an island

where no people lived, only bears.

There were black bears and

brown bears,

polar bears and grizzly bears.

Bears of all sizes

bears of all shapes,

bears of all colors

bears of all weights.

3

Bear Island was lovely

with beautiful streams,

that ran from the mountains

straight down to the seas.

The landscape was covered
with grass and with forest
and the birds and the crickets
sang for hours in chorus.

The sky was clear blue
almost all of the time,
the days passed by slowly
and the bears felt just fine.

The bears loved to wander
all around their island home,
each bear free to roam
where it wanted to roam.

Bears rolled in the grass
and climbed up the trees,
they played in the water
and watched honey bees.

Whenever a bear
would feel hunger pull,
to a stream it would amble
and eat fish until full.

No fish ever was wasted,

no bear took more than its need,

for the streams were always there

and a bear could always feed.

The bears lived together
in small packs here and there,
they ate and they slept
and made more baby bears.

They looked out at the stars
from inside of their dens,
and pondered their purpose
as they moved 'cross the heavens.

Bear life was simple
and bear life was good,
nature controlled things
and all worked as it should.

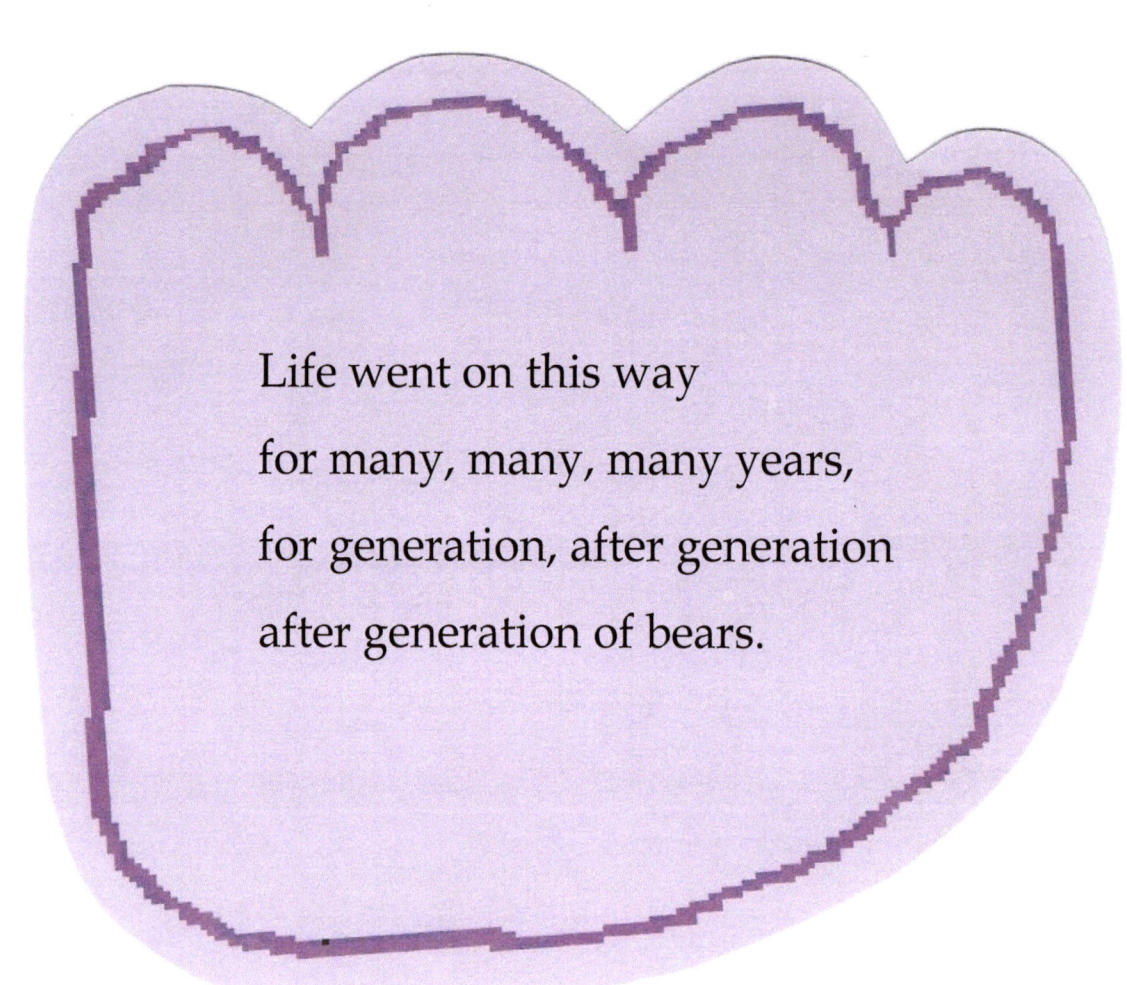

Life went on this way

for many, many, many years,

for generation, after generation

after generation of bears.

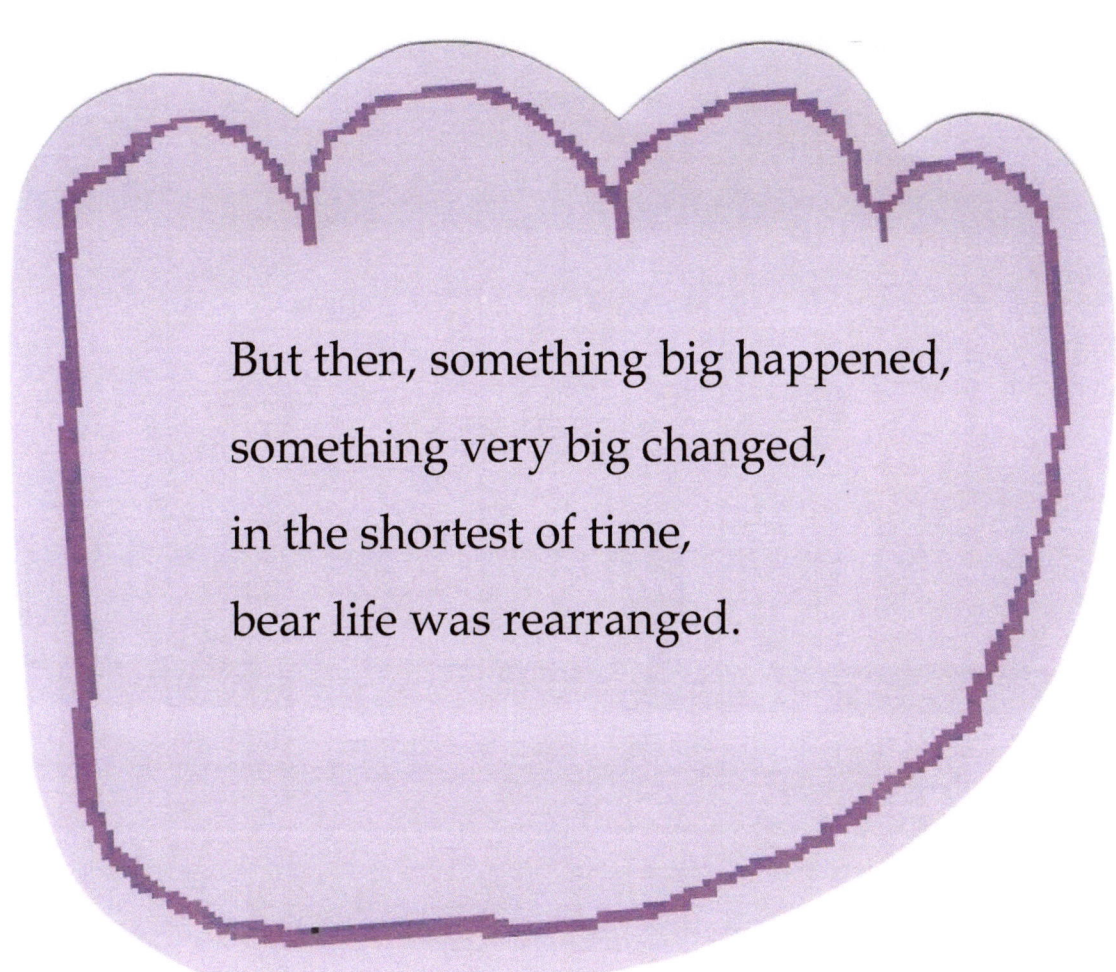

But then, something big happened,

something very big changed,

in the shortest of time,

bear life was rearranged.

What happened was this . . .

A few bears caught extra fish —
much more than they could eat,
they'd found a way to store them
by smoking and curing the meat.

These bears were so happy
they could eat from their store,
in times when fish were scarce,
they wouldn't go hungry anymore.

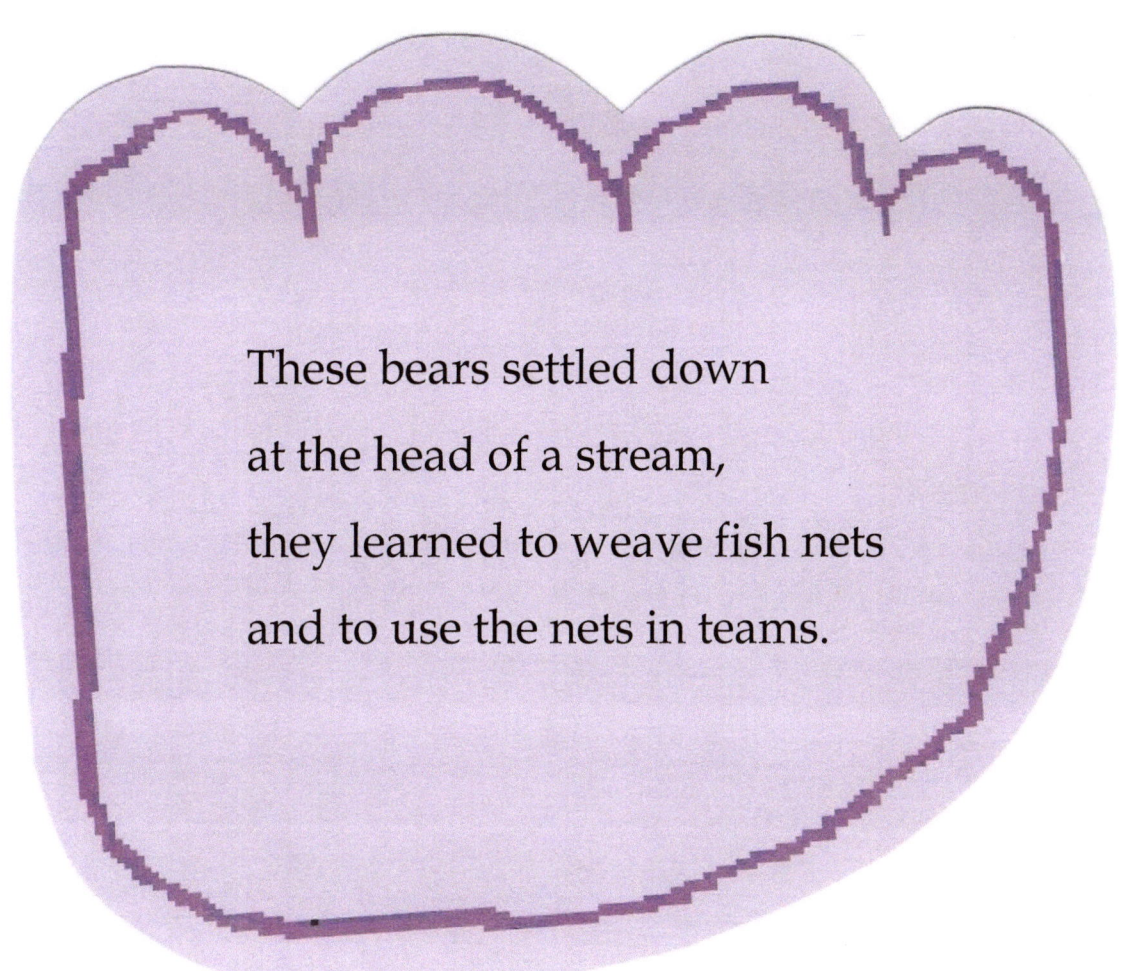

These bears settled down

at the head of a stream,

they learned to weave fish nets

and to use the nets in teams.

19

They built a bear town
the first bear town ever,
they made many new things
these bears were quite clever.

They made houses out of wood
and ovens out of clay,
they wrote themselves an alphabet
and began performing plays.

They learned how to fashion

copper, bronze, and iron ore,

into jewelry and axes . . .

and locks for their doors.

Soon some of the other bears

saw these bears up the stream,

saw their houses of wood

saw their trinkets that gleamed.

These bears liked what they saw
and they too wanted a town,
so they too found a stream
and they too settled down.

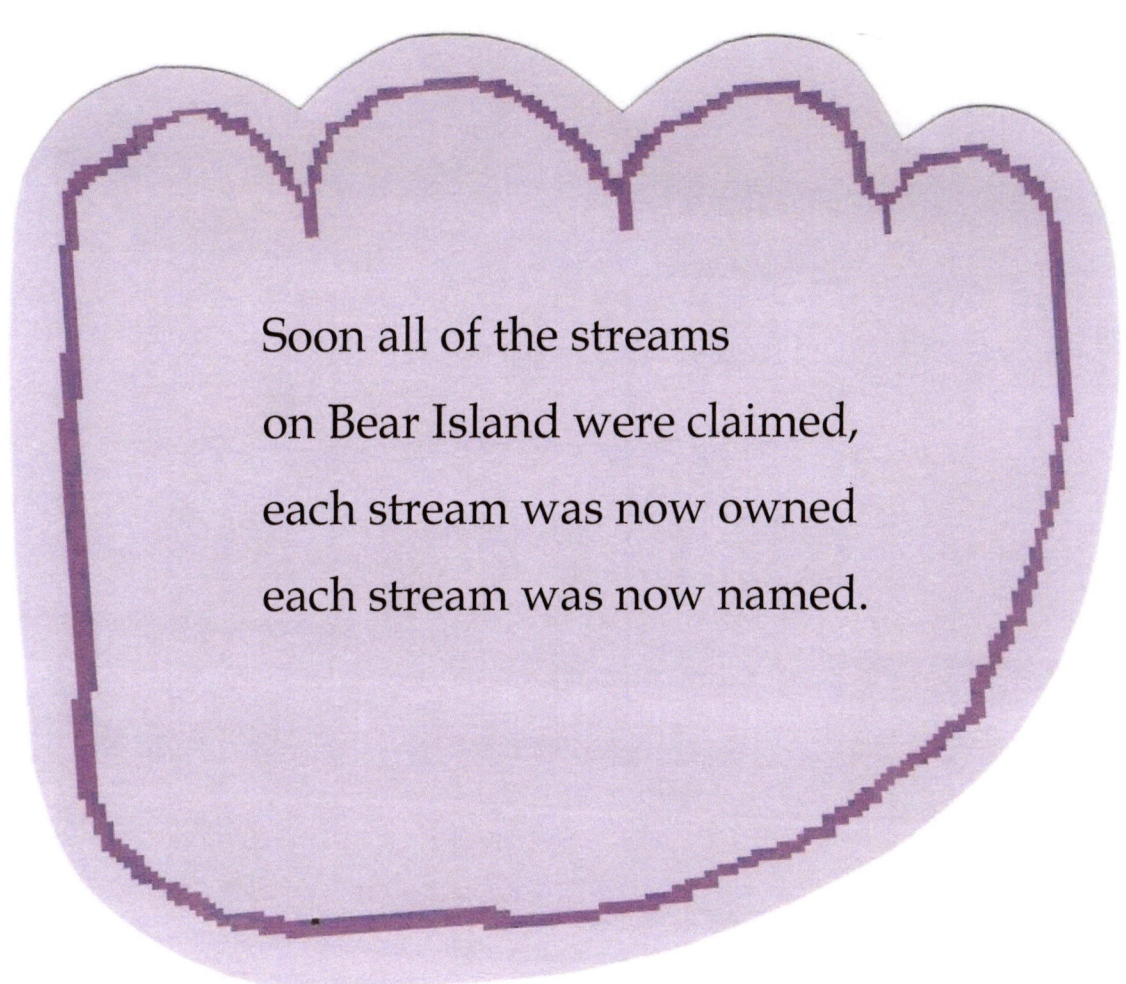

Soon all of the streams

on Bear Island were claimed,

each stream was now owned

each stream was now named.

The bears in these towns
were happy indeed,
they had conquered the streams
and met all their own needs.

26

They had stored so much fish
that it was up to the rafters,
they could never eat it all
before going to the hereafter.

So they wrote down a law
passing wealth to their heirs,
so each family forever
could keep what was theirs.

But soon the bears down the stream
started feeling the squeeze,
as the upstream bears caught more
those downstream had no feed.

They asked the upstream bears
to let some fish past their nets,
but this plea for a share
with anger was met.

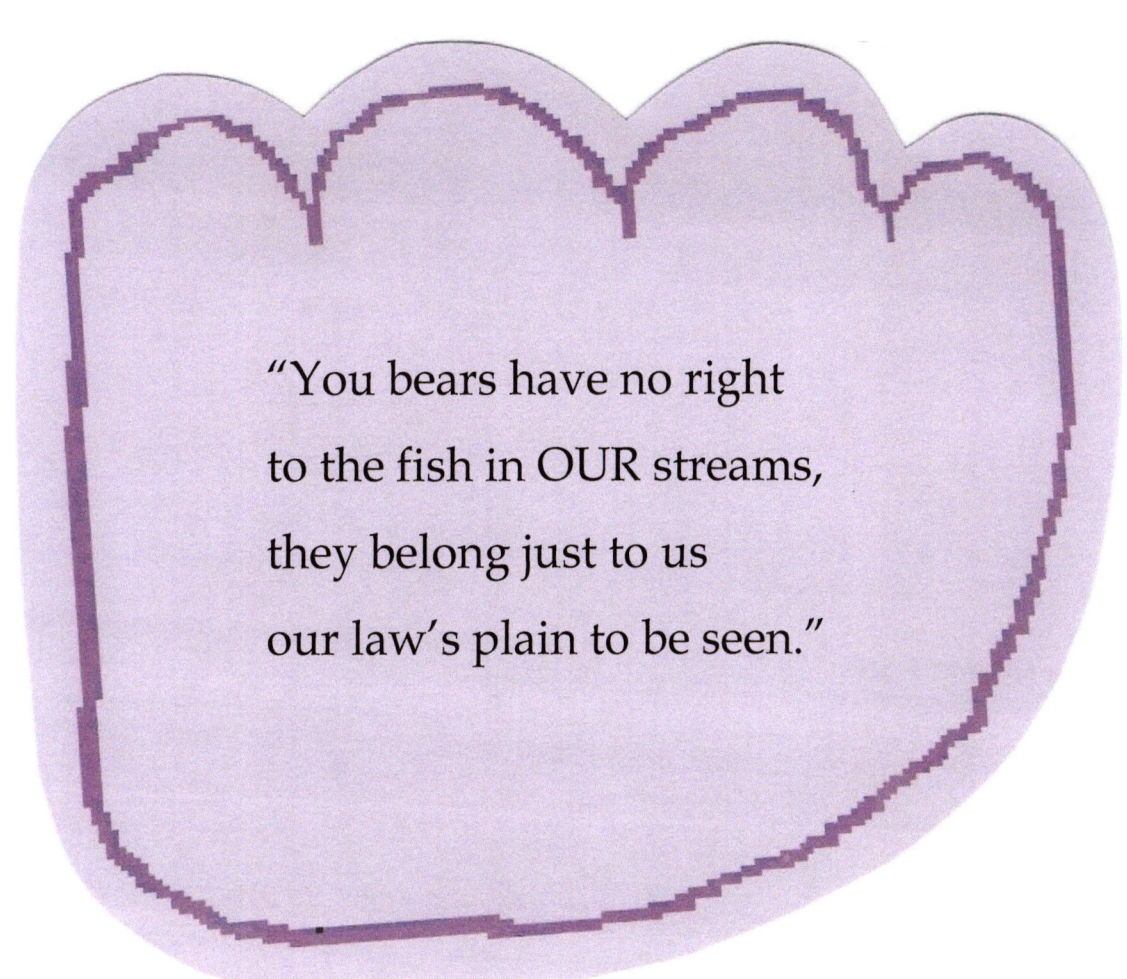

"You bears have no right
to the fish in OUR streams,
they belong just to us
our law's plain to be seen."

Now the bears down the stream

were in quite a spot,

Bear Island was divided

between the have and have nots.

The downstream bears had to work

for what those upstream would give,

they had no other choice really

they had no other way to live.

And soon the bears up the stream

claimed they owned all the ground,

and they made it a crime

to go roaming around.

Most bears were not happy
bear life was a strain,
even those up the stream
could be heard to complain.

Police bears were needed
to guard treasures and homes,
from those they called criminals
who would steal all they owned.

Bear Island ran on ugly things
on hoarding and on greed,
bears fought against other bears
bears made other bears bleed.

But then another change happened,
and this was big indeed . . .

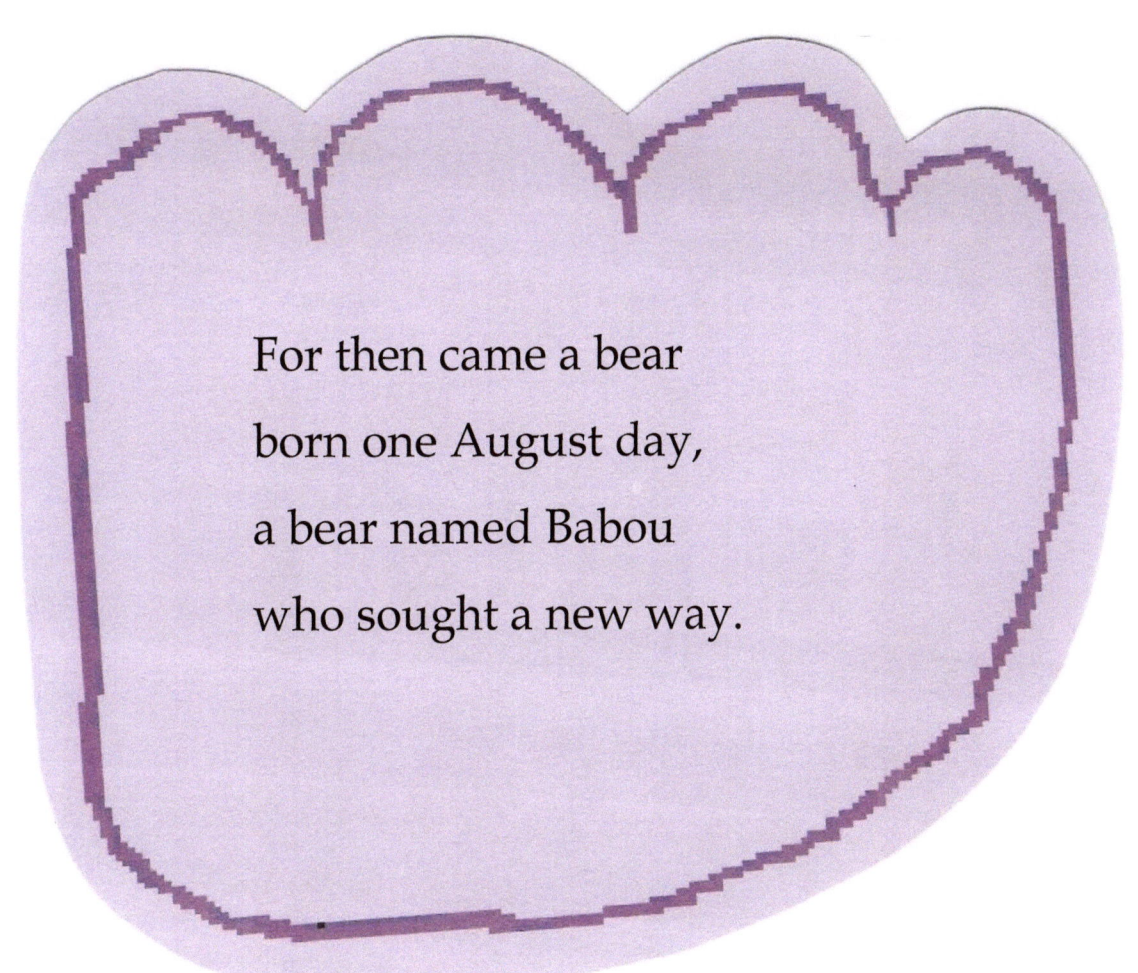

For then came a bear

born one August day,

a bear named Babou

who sought a new way.

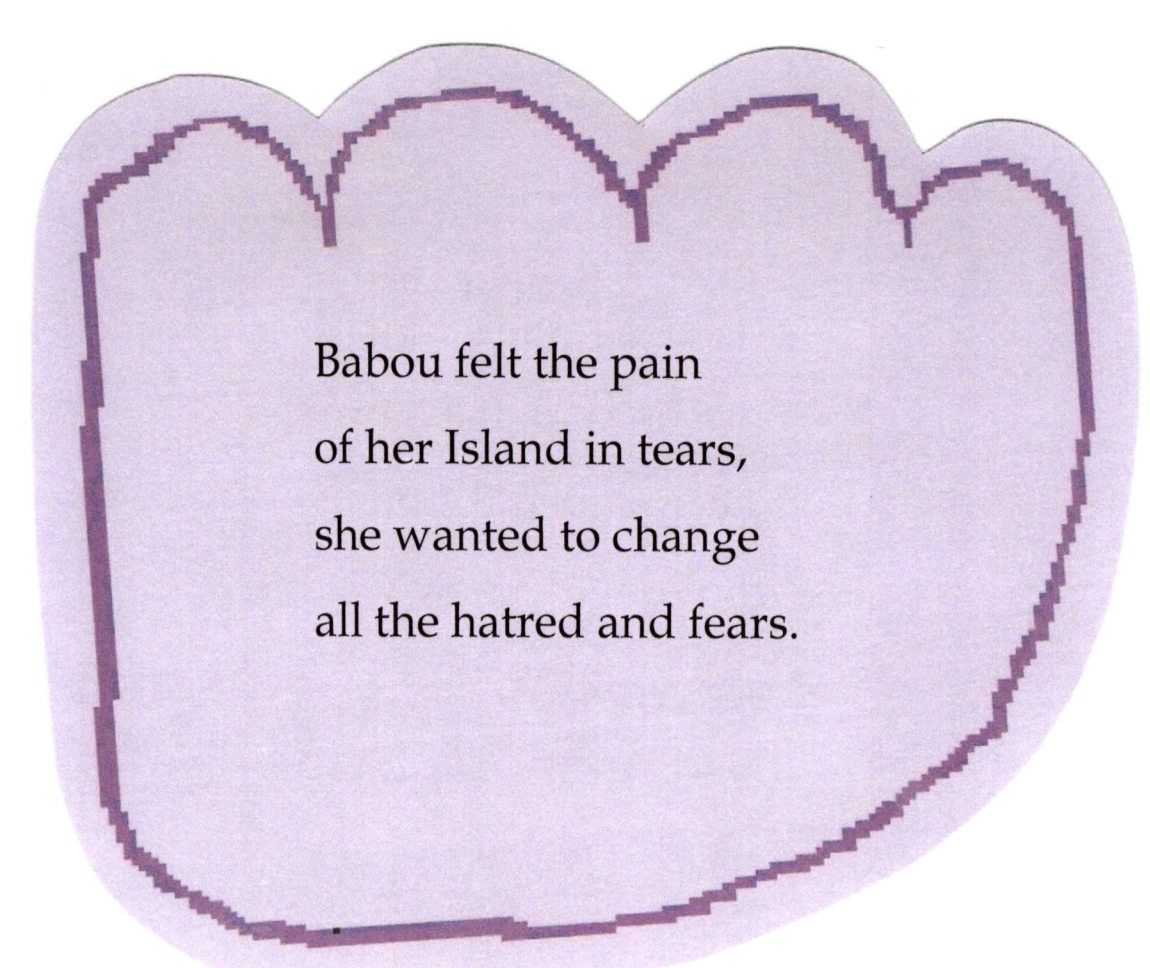

Babou felt the pain
of her Island in tears,
she wanted to change
all the hatred and fears.

She climbed to the top
of the mountain most high,
and reached to the heavens
and started to cry.

"Show me a way," she called
"to change my Island's fate,
a new way of living,
an end to this hate."

A pillar of light
poured down from above,
it touched Babou softly
and she felt a great love.

43

She looked at her hands
and saw they were aglow,
with the light that had touched her
the light seemed to flow.

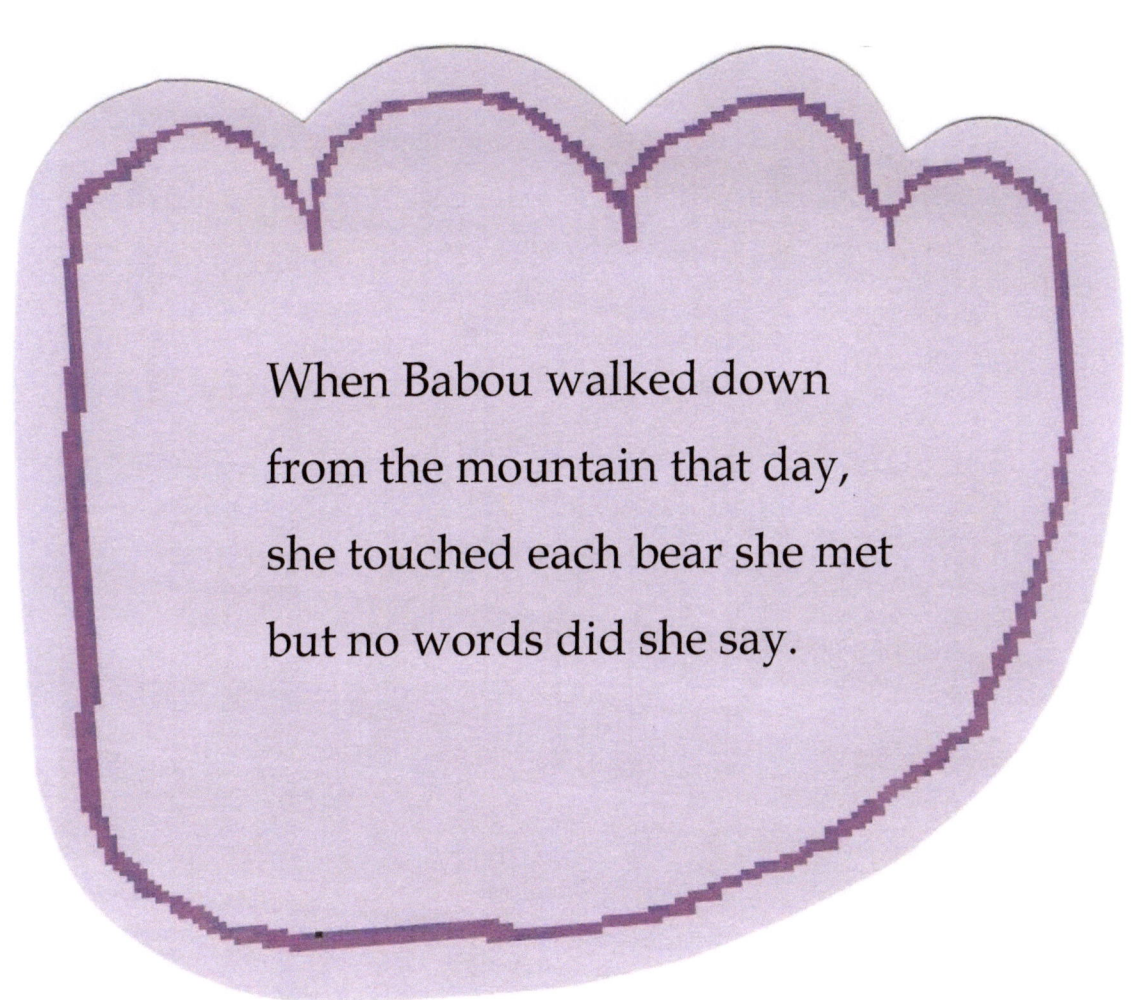

When Babou walked down
from the mountain that day,
she touched each bear she met
but no words did she say.

And each bear who was touched
felt the peace of that love,
and when they touched another
love passed glove to glove.

46

Soon each bear on Bear Island

had been touched by the light,

and each bear on Bear Island

somehow knew what was right.

Each bear on Bear Island

started to care,

and each bear on Bear Island

started to share.

THE END

Copyright 2000

Monica Wallach

www.BabouTheBear.com

www.ingramcontent.com/pod-product-compliance
Lightning Source LLC
Chambersburg PA
CBHW040959170626
46815CB00002B/79